"I can't believe she did it"

MICHELLE

Michelle is totally shocked by the letter she reads in her favorite advice column, *Dear Libby*. It's about someone who can't stand her little sister—from a girl that sounds exactly like Stephanie!

Michelle is convinced that Stephanie wrote the letter. Now she's got to find a way to make her sister like her again—no matter what it takes.

STEPHANIE

Stephanie is excited for the Challenge Day contest at John Muir Middle School. She's sure her team will win the prize for best art sculpture. But Grant Munsen, captain of another Challenge Team, tells Sephanie *he's* going to win.

Stephanie's ready to prove him wrong—or she would be, if Michelle didn't mess up all of her plans! Michelle says she's just trying to be nice, but Stephanie's not so sure. Just whose side is her sister on, anyway?

FULL HOUSE™: SISTERS books

Available from MINSTREL Books

FULL HOUSE™
Sisters

Ask Miss Know-It-All

SUZANNE WEYN

A Parachute Press Book

A
MINSTREL®
BOOK

Published by POCKET BOOKS
New York   London   Toronto   Sydney   Singapore

A MINSTREL PAPERBACK *Original*

A Minstrel Book published by
POCKET BOOKS, a division of Simon & Schuster, Inc.
1230 Avenue of the Americas, New York, NY 10020

A PARACHUTE PRESS BOOK

Copyright © and ™ 2000 by Warner Bros.

ISBN: 0-671-04090-1

First Minstrel Books printing November 2000

10 9 8 7 6 5 4 3 2 1

A MINSTREL BOOK and colophon are registered trademarks of Simon & Schuster, Inc.

Printed in the U.S.A.

Michelle

Chapter
1

Hey, Michelle, catch!"

A football sailed across the living room toward nine-year-old Michelle Tanner after she closed the front door Friday afternoon. She caught it and expertly passed it back to her tall, slim father, Danny.

"You're just in time." Her father smiled at her. "We're starting an after-school game of touch football."

Michelle's uncle Jesse hurried down the stairs. "Ready to throw the old ball around?" he asked her, pulling a 49ers hat over his thick, dark hair.

"Sorry. I can't," Michelle replied. She plunked her backpack down on the stairs. "Cassie and Mandy are coming over." Cassie Wilkens and Mandy Metz were Michelle's two best friends.

"They can play, too," Danny insisted.

Joey Gladstone jogged in from the kitchen wearing a football helmet, uniform, and full padding. "Hey, cool! Did I hear that Michelle and her pals are joining us out in the back-yard?" he asked.

Michelle laughed at Joey's outfit.

Uncle Jesse and Joey, Danny's best friend, had lived at the Tanners' house since Michelle's mother died, when Michelle was just a baby. They had helped Danny raise his three daughters—Michelle and her big sisters, Stephanie, who was thirteen, and D.J., who was eighteen. Everyone in the family had lots of fun living together.

Then, a few years ago, Uncle Jesse had mar-ried Aunt Becky, and the two moved into an attic apartment in the house. A couple of years after that the two of them had adorable twin boys, Alex and Nicky. That made nine people living in one very full house. Comet, their golden retriever, made ten.

"Sorry, guys, I don't think Cassie and Mandy will want to play," Michelle told Uncle Jesse and Joey. "We planned to go out for ice cream. Mandy's mom is going to drive us. This will be the first time we've seen each other outside of school in a couple of weeks."

Michelle couldn't believe how busy she and her friends had been lately. Mandy had been practicing every day for a big tennis tournament. It had taken up nearly all her time. Cassie was in the school choir. She'd been super busy with rehearsals until last weekend, when the chorus finally had their concert.

All of Michelle's time had been taken up by being a volunteer at a community art show at the library. She helped hang pictures all week and even had some of her own artwork on display.

But finally, all their activities had slowed down—for now. At last they'd have time to do some fun things together.

"Suit yourself," Joey said. "But you'll be missing a great game."

"Next time," Michelle promised.

Danny tossed the football to Joey. "Let's get going," Danny said. "See you later, Michelle."

As they left for the backyard, Michelle grabbed her backpack and headed upstairs to the bedroom she shared with Stephanie. "Steph?" she called as she entered the room. No one was inside.

Ahhh! Michelle thought. *A minute to myself.* She dropped her backpack onto her bed and glanced around the room. Hey, the new issue of *Daisy* magazine was here. Michelle spied it on Stephanie's twin bed.

Daisy was the absolute coolest girl's magazine ever. Stephanie and Michelle shared a subscription. Both of them looked forward to reading it every month.

Michelle eagerly scooped up the magazine. A crease in the front cover told her that Stephanie had already looked at it. *She must have come in and gone out again*, Michelle realized.

4

Flopping on her own bed, Michelle began turning the pages of the magazine. *Daisy* always made her smile. It was full of jokes, cool fashions, interesting articles, and short stories. She glanced over an article on funky ways to decorate jeans. Then she turned to one of her favorite features, "Dear Libby."

Every month girls wrote to Libby for advice. Michelle always loved Libby's answers. They made perfect sense, and Michelle was sure they helped the readers solve their problems.

Michelle checked out the first letter printed in the column. A girl who signed herself "Lonely" said she hadn't made any friends since she moved to a new town.

Libby's advice was to be patient. Making new friends took time. *That's true,* Michelle thought. Then Libby gave the girl some hints for meeting people. Michelle nodded to herself. *Libby did a good job handling that one.*

The second letter was from a girl whose best friend had a new best friend. *That* is *a tough problem,* Michelle thought.

Libby told the girl to make some new friends herself while remaining friendly with the old best friend. That way, she wouldn't feel like she was losing a best friend, but gaining a whole bunch of new friends. *That makes sense*, Michelle agreed. *Libby's two for two.*

She started on the third letter.

Dear Libby,
Even though I live in a big house, it is very crowded. Relatives and even some people who are not related to us live with me and my family. Besides that, we have a big dog. It's a zoo here.

Michelle smiled. Talk about a situation she could relate to! It almost sounded as if the girl writing the letter was living in *her* house! She continued reading.

The worst part is that I have to share my room with my sister. I can't stand her. She is the ultimate pain. I don't think I can

live with her another minute without losing my mind. What should I do?
Signed, Desperate

Michelle frowned. Wait a minute. This girl
sounded even more familiar than she thought.
She put the magazine on her lap and stared at
the third letter. Her mind raced, clicking off
the facts.

This girl lived in a crowded household—with
relatives, friends, and a dog. Plus, she shared a
room with her sister. There was only one person
Michelle knew who fit a description like that.

"Oh, no! *Stephanie* wrote this," Michelle
said to herself.

Stephanie had to have written it, she reasoned. After all, what were the chances that
some other girl had a life nearly identical to
hers? The answer was: pretty slim.

Chewing her lower lip, Michelle kept staring at the letter. Did Stephanie really think of
her as *the ultimate pain?*

Michelle didn't want to believe it. But there
it was—in black and white!

"Finally, the three of us are together!" a voice sang out from the doorway. Michelle looked up to see Cassie stepping into the room. "Hi, Michelle. Your dad let us in," she called.

Mandy followed Cassie into the room. "My mom's outside and we're ready to—" Mandy stopped short. "Hey, what's the matter?" she asked.

"Yeah, you look bummed, Michelle," Cassie agreed. "Is something wrong?"

Michelle nodded. Tears brimmed in her eyes as she shoved the magazine toward them. "Look at the third letter," she said.

Mandy took the issue and began to read. Cassie gazed down at the article over her shoulder.

In a minute Mandy looked up at Michelle. "I don't get it. Why are you upset about this?"

"Can't you tell who wrote it?" Michelle demanded.

Both girls shook their heads.

"It's Stephanie!" Michelle told them. "Who else could it be?"

8

Mandy sat on the edge of the bed, beside Michelle. Her eyebrows were knit together thoughtfully. "Well . . . there are a lot of things that are the same about this girl and Stephanie," she admitted. "But this girl can't stand her sister."

Cassie joined them on the bed, putting the magazine on her lap. "Yeah, you and Stephanie get along great," she pointed out. "Sure, you argue sometimes. But all sisters do that."

"Besides," Mandy continued. "Stephanie's never acted like she doesn't like you—right?"

"Right." Michelle flopped back. "But what if, all this time, she's been hiding her true feelings about me? What if she really hates me?"

Michelle suddenly felt a tightness in her chest. She realized that she really wanted to cry.

Mandy sighed. "Well, what did Libby tell the girl in the letter to do?" she asked.

Michelle realized she didn't know. She hadn't read that part yet. Picking up the *Daisy* issue, she flipped back to "Dear Libby."

" 'There are two things that you can do,' "
Michelle read the answer aloud. " 'You can try
being extra nice to your sister. Maybe she'll
take the hint and be nicer in return. If that
fails, try staying away from your sister as
much as you can. If you get some space from
her, maybe she won't seem so bad.' "

"I guess that's good advice," Mandy said.

"It is," Michelle agreed.

"Maybe Stephanie will start being extra
nice to you now," Cassie suggested. "That's
what Libby told her to do."

"Uh-uh. I'm not waiting for Stephanie,"
Michelle said. She leaped up from the bed.
"*I'll* be super nice to *her* first! That way she'll
see what a thoughtful sister I really am—and
then she'll like me again."

"Great," Mandy said. She grabbed Michelle's
hand and dragged her toward the door. "You
can start by bringing her back some ice cream
from the ice-cream parlor."

"Yes!" Michelle cheered. Then she frowned.
"But wait. I don't have enough money for two
ice creams."

"Too bad," Cassie sympathized. "But I'm sure we can think of something else you can do by the time we get back."

"No. You've given me a great idea," Michelle said. "Stephanie's favorite dessert is Rocky Road pudding. Dad bought all the ingredients but no one has had time to make it."

"So, you'll make it when you get home," Cassie said.

"There won't be time when I get back," Michelle explained. "I'll have to make it right now so it will be set for supper tonight."

Yes! This was a really great plan, Michelle decided. And it couldn't wait. "You guys go without me," she told her friends.

"But—it won't be the same," Mandy wailed. "The whole idea was for the three of us to do something together."

"Please?" Michelle asked in a small voice. "You have to understand." She snapped her fingers as another idea came to her. "I know. We'll just reschedule our best-friend day! Come over here tomorrow. I just got a funny new video. The three of us can watch it together."

"It's not what we planned, but it sounds okay," Mandy said, giving in.

"Great," Michelle agreed. "Now you guys go have fun and I'll get to work on that pudding."

She walked her friends to the front door, waved good-bye, and headed into the kitchen.

Michelle gathered the ingredients for Rocky Road pudding from the pantry, and placed each one on the counter, "Let's see . . . marshmallows, graham crackers, chocolate chips, instant pudding." Looked like she had everything.

"Hey, Michelle." Danny walked in from the backyard. He took a glass from the cupboard and poured himself some water. "Where are Cassie and Mandy?" he asked.

"I told them to go for ice cream without me," Michelle explained. "I wanted to stay home to make Stephanie's favorite dessert, Rocky Road pudding."

"That's really sweet of you, Michelle,"

Danny said. "But Stephanie's sleeping at Allie's tonight."

Michelle bit her lower lip. *What? Staying over at Allie's?* She remembered Dear Libby's second piece of advice to "Desperate." *Try staying away from your sister as much as you can.*

Oh, no, Michelle thought. *Stephanie hates me so much that she's totally avoiding me! This is much worse than I realized!*

Chapter
2

I am so glad we're having this sleepover tonight," Stephanie told her friends Darcy Powell and Allie Taylor. They were walking along the upper level of the mall together, heading for the food court.

"Why?" Darcy asked as she straightened a sparkly clip in her tight dark curls.

Stephanie sighed. "The strangest thing happened today."

"What?" Allie asked.

Stephanie twirled a strand of her long blond hair before answering. She still couldn't

1 4

actually believe what she'd read that afternoon.

"Do you know *Daisy* magazine?" she asked.

"Sure," Allie answered, nodding.

"Love it," Darcy agreed.

"I'm pretty sure that in this issue there's a letter in 'Dear Libby' written by Michelle."

"What?" Darcy gasped.

"She signed it 'Desperate,' but I just know she's the person who wrote it," Stephanie insisted. "Everything about the letter matches Michelle's description."

"So what was the letter about?" Allie asked, her blue eyes growing wide beneath her light-brown bangs.

"She said that she can't stand the sister she has to share a room with," Stephanie told them. "In other words, she can't stand *me!*" Stephanie frowned deeply, realizing it hurt her to even speak those words. Until today when she had read the letter, she had no idea Michelle felt that way about her.

But now she had to face facts. After all, it was right there in the magazine.

"No way," Darcy argued. "Michelle doesn't hate you. She adores you."

"Totally," Allie agreed.

Stephanie shook her head. "Not according to the letter in 'Dear Libby.' "

"All right. Say—just *say*—that Michelle *did* write that letter," Allie said, "What do you plan to do about it?"

"Libby advised the writer either to be extra nice to her sister, or to give her a lot of space," Stephanie replied. "I figured that advice would be good for me as well as for Michelle."

She shrugged. "So, from now on, I'm giving her some space. That's why I'm so glad I'll be sleeping over tonight. Michelle will have our room all to herself. Maybe it will make her feel better."

"Maybe she'll miss you," Allie said. "Then she'll realize what a great sister you are."

"I hope so," Stephanie replied.

The smell of greasy French fries wafted past Stephanie's nose. They'd finally reached the food court. She glanced around and saw that, as usual, it was crowded with kids she and her friends knew from John Muir Middle School.

"I say we go for pizza," Darcy suggested.

"Sounds good," Stephanie agreed.

"Hey, that reminds me about our Social Studies project," Allie began as they walked to the counter. "Do we have everything ready for our written report?"

"Wait—pizza reminds you of ancient Egypt?" Darcy asked.

Allie grinned. "Sure. A slice of pizza is the same shape as a pyramid, isn't it?"

Stephanie and Darcy laughed. *Sometimes Allie is just too funny*, Stephanie thought.

Last week Stephanie, Allie, and Darcy had built a miniature pyramid at Darcy's house. This past weekend they had made a poster about King Tut at Allie's house. Tomorrow they planned to finish up the written report at Stephanie's house. The whole project was coming together great. Stephanie definitely saw an A in their future.

"I think we're all set to start the written report this weekend," Stephanie told her friends. "I got all the books we'll need from the library a couple of weeks ago."

"Way to go," Darcy cheered. "I hear they're all checked out and no one can find books on Egypt anywhere."

"That's why *I* got them early." Stephanie waggled her eyebrows at her friend. "I've read through them and marked the important parts with colored Post-its."

Stephanie gave her order. The attendant handed her back a slice and a soda, which she paid for.

"You've marked the pages with Post-its already? Amazing. This report is going to be a snap," Allie said.

Darcy frowned, gazing around the seating area. "There are so many people from John Muir here, I feel like I'm in the cafeteria," she remarked. The three friends looked around for an empty table. After a minute they found one and sat down to eat.

"Thanks for doing all that work ahead of time, Steph," Darcy said between bites. "You are so organized. No wonder the kids in our Challenge group voted you team captain."

Stephanie smiled at the compliment. John

Muir Middle School was having a special Challenge Day that was going to begin the next day, Saturday. Anyone in Stephanie's grade who wanted to participate could. The kids had been broken up into groups—with a captain for each group.

The groups were being challenged to create a piece of art. The winning piece would be displayed at John Muir for an entire year.

"Speaking of Challenge Day, look who's sitting over there," Allie said. She nodded in the direction of a red-haired boy sitting across the food court with two guy friends.

Stephanie frowned. It was Grant Munsen. Like Stephanie, he was heading one of the Challenge groups.

"Doesn't he make you mad?" Allie asked.

"Definitely," Stephanie agreed. "He's so stuck on himself."

"He's cute, though," Darcy mentioned.

"Ugh! No way!" Stephanie wrinkled her nose in disgust. "All Grant ever talks about is how he's the smartest kid at school, the most athletic, and the best-looking."

"I know." Allie rolled her eyes in agreement.

"Even if he was a total babe he'd be completely unattractive with that kind of attitude," Stephanie insisted.

"You always say just the right thing to knock him off his pedestal, though." Darcy laughed.

Stephanie smiled. "Somebody's got to stand up to him. That's why he doesn't like me. Not that I care what he thinks."

"His entire Challenge group is acting just like he does," Darcy added. "They're going around the school saying they're sure to win Challenge Day."

"Let them talk." Stephanie cautiously glanced over her shoulder at Grant's table before she went on. "I wanted to talk to you guys first before I talk to the others. I know we had decided on a project, but I have a new idea that I think is great. One that could make us the winners of Challenge Day."

Darcy and Allie leaned closer. "Spill," Allie whispered.

"Why don't we build a really big sculpture

using only recycled materials? The art will be totally earth-conscious." Stephanie looked at her friends to see what they thought.

"Excellent," Darcy said slowly. "It shows school spirit by being aware of our role in the environment."

"If the other seven members of our team agree to change from making a mural, I think it's a great idea," Allie chimed in.

"I was thinking it could be something abstract—you know, not completely realistic looking," Stephanie explained.

"Awesome," Allie said. "Let Grant Munsen try to beat that!" She suddenly slapped her hand over her mouth.

"What?" Stephanie and Darcy asked at the same time.

"Grant and his friends are behind us," she whispered, lifting the hand from her mouth.

Stephanie whirled around. She hadn't seen Grant and his two friends switch tables. They *were* right behind her—only one table away.

"I hope they didn't hear our idea," Stephanie said, worried.

"They couldn't have," Darcy insisted.

"Oh, no, they're coming over," Allie reported with a groan.

Grant led the way. His two friends hung back a little, but Grant came right up to their table. "Hey, girls, what's up?"

Stephanie studied him. With his red hair and gray eyes, he was definitely good-looking. It was too bad his personality destroyed his looks.

"If you must know, we were planning an awesome project for Challenge Day," Darcy told him.

Stephanie bumped Darcy's foot with her own. She didn't want Darcy to give anything away.

"You might as well not bother," Grant told them. "My group has a project so awesome it will blow away all the competition."

"Really?" Stephanie raised her eyebrows. "I happen to think our project is pretty awesome, too."

Grant laughed. "You may think that, but you have no idea what you're up against."

Oooh! Stephanie felt her face flush red. Why was Grant always so annoying! She stood up. "Maybe you don't know what *you're* up against."

"Don't make me laugh," Grant scoffed.

"You might as well laugh now, while you still can," she said scornfully. "Because you won't be too happy after *we* win."

"Do you want to bet on that?" Grant replied, stepping closer.

"No, but my team is winning. Count on it!"

Stephanie turned and noticed Allie's and Darcy's surprised faces. All at once she realized she'd been shouting. She glanced around and saw that all the kids from John Muir Middle School were staring at her, listening to her whole exchange with Grant.

How embarrassing! But she couldn't let Grant see how mortified she felt. That would only make things worse.

Grant quirked his mouth to one side. "The only thing I'm counting on is winning," he said. He turned on his heel and walked away with his friends.

Stephanie sat back down. "Oh, wow," she whispered to her friends. "I can't believe how loud I shouted. Everyone heard me tell Grant we were going to win, didn't they?"

Darcy and Allie nodded. "Uh-huh!"

Stephanie took a deep breath. "Great. We have to win now," she said. "Or I'll look like a total loser!"

Michelle

Chapter
3

Saturday morning a car door slammed outside Michelle's house. Michelle sat up straight, listening. The sound of footsteps came up the walk. *Yes!* She hopped up off the couch. *It must be Stephanie coming home from her sleepover.* Michelle wanted to be the one to open the door for her.

She put on her biggest, most welcoming smile and peered out the small window beside the door.

"We're back," Mandy sang out, catching sight of Michelle. Cassie stood beside her.

Michelle's smile faded. She'd forgotten her plan to watch a video with her friends. "Oh, hi," she murmured. "Come in."

"Thanks for the happy greeting!" Mandy joked.

"Sorry," Michelle said. "I was hoping you were Stephanie. I wanted to do something nice for her by letting her in."

"How about you do something nice for *us* by putting in the video," Cassie said. She flopped onto the couch.

"Microwave popcorn wouldn't hurt, either," Mandy added.

"Sure. Okay," Michelle agreed. She took the video from its case and popped it into the VCR.

Coming attractions filled the TV screen. Mandy settled onto the couch beside Cassie. "You don't have to get popcorn, Michelle," she said. "I don't want you to miss any of the—"

"Hold on," Michelle cut her off. Her dad was coming down the stairs. She really needed to talk to him.

Michelle punched Pause on the VCR. "Hang on a sec," she said to her friends. "I need to talk to my dad."

Danny stopped by the front door. "What's up, Michelle?" he asked.

Michelle took hold of his arm and guided him out to the front porch. She needed some privacy. "I have an important question, Dad," she began. "Can you think of something really nice I could do for Stephanie?"

Danny arched one eyebrow. "Why do you suddenly want to be extra nice to Stephanie?" he asked.

Michelle's mind raced. Should she tell her dad about Stephanie's letter in *Daisy?*

No, she decided. Danny didn't like it when his daughters fought. He might yell at Stephanie for writing the letter. Then Stephanie would like Michelle even less.

"Uh—no reason," Michelle fibbed. "She's just such a great sister that I want to do something special for her."

Danny placed a hand on his chin. Michelle knew that meant he was thinking. He gazed around on the porch. Then his eyes fixed on Stephanie's bike. "You could wash her bike," he suggested. "Make it all nice and shiny for her."

Michelle wanted to chuckle. Leave it to her totally neat father to think of a surprise that involved cleaning.

"I *could*," she agreed. "But somehow, that doesn't seem special enough." It was already November, Michelle reasoned. Soon it would be too cold for Stephanie to take out her bike. Washing it now seemed silly.

Danny glanced at his watch. "Well, I've got to get to the bank before it closes. Uncle Jesse and Aunt Becky are upstairs with the twins if you need them. And don't worry, I'll keep thinking of nice things to do for your sister, okay?" Danny said.

"Great, thanks," Michelle replied. She walked back into the house.

"Finally. Can we watch the movie now?" Mandy asked as soon as Michelle had closed the front door.

"Sure." Michelle hit Play. The video began

again. Michelle plopped down on the couch next to Allie.

The movie was a comedy. Mandy and Cassie cracked up beside her, but Michelle wasn't really paying attention. She was too busy worrying about Stephanie.

"Oh, this is too funny," Cassie gasped with laughter. She fell into Michelle's arm. "Look! Look! His wig is *on fire!*"

"What? Oh, yeah," Michelle said. "Funny."

Cassie frowned at her. "Aren't you watching the movie?"

"Of course I am," Michelle replied. "It's hysterical."

"Then why aren't you laughing?" Mandy asked.

"I *am* laughing," Michelle insisted. "On the inside."

"Hey, girls," Uncle Jesse greeted them as he crossed the living room. He was heading into the kitchen.

Uncle Jesse! Michelle thought. He was really smart. Maybe he could think of something she could do for Stephanie. She jumped up from the couch and went to the kitchen.

"Don't you want to see the movie?" Mandy asked.

"Yes. I'm . . . uh . . . getting the popcorn," Michelle said quickly.

Cassie picked up the remote control clicker. "I'll pause it until you come back," she offered. "That way you won't miss anything."

"Thanks," Michelle said. She ducked into the kitchen. Uncle Jesse was stooped over, staring into the refrigerator.

"Yuck. Nothing but healthy stuff," he grumbled.

"Uncle Jesse," Michelle began. "I'd like to do something special for Stephanie, but I can't think of what to do."

"I know the perfect thing!" Uncle Jesse answered as he shut the refrigerator. "How about making her a batch of those brownies you made last week? Only this time, smother them in chocolate icing and then add pieces of chocolate inside. Stephanie would love that."

"Wait a minute," Michelle said, folding her arms. "Aren't brownies *your* favorite dessert?"

"Are they?" Uncle Jesse asked with a mischievous grin on his face.

Michelle nodded. "They are. Besides, I want to do something better for her than just make a dessert."

"I don't know, Michelle. Desserts are pretty special." Uncle Jesse patted his stomach.

Michelle sighed. When Uncle Jesse was hungry, he was absolutely no help. "Thanks anyway," she told him.

She went back into the living room. "Hey! Where's the popcorn?" Mandy asked.

"Oops," Michelle said. "I forgot to make it."

"Then what were you doing in there all that time?" Allie asked.

"Um . . . talking to Uncle Jesse." Michelle knew Cassie and Mandy were expecting a special "friends only" day. They'd be upset if they knew she was still worrying about Stephanie. She decided not to tell them. "Put on the movie. I'll be back in a flash with popcorn."

Michelle ran back to the kitchen, zapped

the microwave popcorn, and brought it to the living room.

Mandy and Allie were laughing so hard they were holding on to each other. "What happened?" Michelle asked, sitting down with the bowl of popcorn on her lap.

"Well, this guy went up the tree to get his wig," Allie explained. "Then a bird came along and sat in it. And it was a bird he sort of knew because it used to belong to his neighbor . . ."

"It's hard to explain," Mandy put in. Using the remote, she hit Rewind. "I'll play it back so you know what's going on."

As the film rewound, Joey came in the front door. *Yes! Joey will know what I can do for Stephanie,* Michelle thought. He was always full of good ideas. She handed Cassie the popcorn. "Bathroom!" she called out, then followed Joey up the stairs.

"Joey," she called when they got into the hallway. "Can I ask you something?"

"Shoot, Michelle," Joey said with a smile.

"I need to come up with something really

nice to do for Stephanie. Do you have any ideas?"

Joey tapped his forehead as he thought. "I know!" he said. "You could do all her homework for the rest of the year. That would be extra-super nice!"

"Joey!" Michelle groaned. "Stephanie's older than me. I haven't learned the stuff she's doing. I wouldn't be able to do her homework."

"Oh, that's right," Joey said. "I forgot."

"Besides, that would be cheating. Now, be serious," she pleaded.

"Okay. Why don't you . . . save up to buy her *a new car?*" Joey exclaimed in his best game-show-host voice.

"That would take about a zillion years," Michelle replied. "And Stephanie's too young to drive, anyway!"

"Sorry, kiddo. I guess I don't have any good ideas for you." He paused. "Why don't you try just being as sweet as you are. You're always nice to everyone."

Michelle forced a weak smile. "Thanks for the advice," she said.

She turned to go back downstairs, and saw a stack of books sitting at the top of the steps. The labels on the book spines told her the whole pile was from the library. A picture of a pyramid was on the cover of the top book.

Michelle remembered that Stephanie had borrowed these books for some project she was doing on ancient Egypt. *But she's had these for an awfully long time*, Michelle thought.

That gave her an idea. She picked up one of the books and opened it to the due date card.

Just as she'd hoped. The books were due back at the library yesterday. Stephanie must have forgotten to return them.

Now she knew what she could do for Stephanie.

Scooping up the rest of the pile, Michelle hurried downstairs. "Come on, you guys," she told Cassie and Mandy. "I have to go somewhere."

"But I just rewound the tape so you could see what you missed," Mandy objected.

"We'll watch it when we come back," Michelle answered. *"Please?"*

"We've been interrupted so many times I don't even know what's going on anymore," Cassie complained.

"I'm sorry. We'll watch it from the very beginning when we come back," Michelle promised.

Mandy and Cassie glanced at each other and shrugged. Cassie clicked off the VCR. "Is this going to take long?" she asked.

"No, but I have to get a ride," Michelle answered.

Uncle Jesse came back into the living room. "Uncle Jesse, I need a ride to the library. Please?" she asked.

He stopped short. "The twins have some picture books that are due back tomorrow— so sure," he agreed. "Just let me get the books and I'll be right back."

Excellent! Michelle pulled on her fleece sweatshirt while Cassie and Mandy threw on their jackets. "What's at the library?" Cassie asked.

"I'm going to return these overdue books for Stephanie," Michelle explained. "It's the perfect nice thing to do for her."

Mandy sighed. "Great. Once we do this will you stop worrying about Stephanie?"

"Yes. Really," Michelle said.

"Thank goodness," Mandy told her. "All you think about anymore is being nice to Stephanie."

"That's because it's important," Michelle insisted.

When Uncle Jesse returned, he drove the girls to the library. There was a short line at the return counter. "Could you return my books, too, while I go upstairs to get new ones for the kids?" Uncle Jesse requested.

"Sure," Michelle agreed. He put the two picture books on the stack of Stephanie's books and headed up to the children's room.

Michelle, Cassie, and Mandy got in the return line. They stood behind a tall, cute red-headed boy.

Somehow, he looked familiar, Michelle thought. Where had she seen him before? The boy turned to glance around the library. *Oh, right!* Michelle remembered. *He's on the John Muir Middle School basketball team.*

Stephanie had taken Michelle to a game with her, and Michelle had had the best time ever. She remembered that this guy was one of the best players on the team. She even remembered his name. "You're Grant, right?"

"That's right," he said, smiling. She could tell he liked that she remembered him.

"I'm Michelle, Stephanie Tanner's sister. I saw you play at a John Muir basketball game. You were awesome!" Michelle explained.

"Thanks," Grant said.

The two picture books slid from the top of Michelle's stack. "Oops!" She giggled.

Grant bent to pick them up for her. As he was putting them back on her pile, he checked out her books on Egypt. "Are you returning those?" he asked.

"Yeah. For Stephanie," she explained.

"You know, I could use those," he told her. "Why don't I return them for you, then I'll check them out for myself."

"There might be an overdue fine," Michelle pointed out.

Grant shrugged. "No problem. It's worth it

to get my hands on these. And this way you won't have to stand in line."

Uncle Jesse joined the girls. "I'll come back with the twins and let them pick a book," he said, explaining his quick return. "There must have been a million screaming five-year-olds up there."

"Great. We don't have to wait in line anymore," Michelle reported. "Grant will return our books for us."

"Excellent," said Uncle Jesse. "Thanks, Grant."

"Oh, no. Thank you," Grant said.

"Now can we go home and watch the movie?" Mandy asked.

"Definitely," Michelle replied. She slung her arms around Cassie and Mandy. "I can't believe how great this turned out. I did a nice, sisterly thing for Stephanie—something she'll totally thank me for—and now I'm going to spend the rest of the afternoon with my two best friends."

Stephanie

Chapter
4

"Will we have to pay for all the stuff?" Allie asked Stephanie that morning on the way to the recycling center.

The night before Stephanie got her group to agree to make the sculpture and they were all going to the center to pick up stuff. Everyone was excited about Stephanie's idea.

"No," Stephanie replied. "The woman I spoke to on the phone said that since we're doing a project for school, the recycling center would donate whatever we need for free."

Stephanie, Allie, and Darcy led the way as

they walked down the street with their Challenge group. Ezra, Kevin, Jessica, Lacey, Matt, Regina, and David—the seven others in the group—followed just steps behind.

All the groups were meeting in the school gym later that day to talk about their projects, but Stephanie had called everyone in her group to meet at Allie's house early that morning to pick up their supplies.

The entire group had agreed to go to the recycling center to gather the materials. After all, they had to be ready to discuss their project that afternoon.

"We should find tons of great material here," Stephanie added. "The woman said to take whatever we want."

They neared the chain-link fence surrounding the center, and suddenly Stephanie stopped short. She couldn't believe what she was seeing. Grant Munsen and his group were *inside* the fence.

"What's going on?" Darcy exclaimed. "What are they doing here?"

"Come on," Stephanie said. "Let's find

out." She stormed through the front entrance and strode right up to Grant.

"Grant! Why is your group here?" she demanded. "What do you think you're doing?"

"What's it look like?" Grant asked with a smirk. "We're gathering materials for our project. It's going to be made entirely from recycled stuff."

"No way! You stole our idea!" Darcy cried.

"I can't believe you would do something so rotten!" Allie added.

"No way," Grant replied. "Who says this is your idea?"

"You heard us talking in the mall yesterday," Stephanie accused. "Admit it."

"What do you think I did, put a secret microphone under your table?" Grant laughed.

By now both sides had gathered to hear what was going on.

"Of course not. But you sneaked up right behind us when we were talking about it. Don't deny it," Stephanie came back at him.

"You're crazy." Grant sneered. "We're here *first* because we had the idea *first*." He paused. "I can't believe your attitude, Stephanie. Just because you thought of something, doesn't mean no one else could have the same idea."

"A-attitude?" Stephanie sputtered. "You're complaining about *my* attitude?" She couldn't believe Grant. He was so arrogant that she wanted to scream. Instead, she turned toward her team members. "Huddle!" she called.

Everyone stood close to her. "Okay, guys," Stephanie whispered to her team. "This is nothing to worry about. Really. Our art project will beat theirs any day. Remember, we're doing an abstract sculpture of this design."

Stephanie unfolded the rough sketch that Allie had drawn last night and showed it to her team again. Everyone studied the design—it was a large shape, similar to a pyramid, with a hole through the middle. "Think about the sculpture and grab as much stuff as you can."

She glanced over her shoulder. Grant's

team was stuffing recycled material into black plastic bags. "Let's go," she told her team.

As quickly as they could, the members of Stephanie's team unfolded the plastic bags they'd brought. Each of them slipped on a pair of heavy-duty work gloves and got down to it.

In about an hour, Stephanie's team had filled their bags. Grant's team was long gone.

Stephanie held an old bike wheel under one arm and grasped an overstuffed garbage bag with the other. "Okay. I think we have everything. We'll have just enough time to get to the gym for the meeting," she said.

When they got to the gym, Stephanie saw that each team had been assigned a work space. Grant and his team were already building, using the materials that they had gathered. Stephanie looked around. She thought this day was supposed to be a planning day, and most of the other groups seemed to be planning still.

Stephanie searched for a clear space for her team to spread out and get to work. The only place available was less than five yards from Grant's team.

Stephanie and her team dragged their recycled materials to the clear space. Grant was busily stacking huge, empty aluminum cans in two side-by-side columns.

"Legs," Allie whispered to Stephanie. "Don't you think? They're making legs."

Stephanie studied the aluminum can columns. Both columns widened at the bottom to become what might be feet. Yup. Those were legs all right.

Grant noticed them staring. "So what are you guys building?" he asked.

"None of your business," she said.

"You have no idea, do you?" Grant taunted her.

"I have a very good idea," Stephanie bluffed. But suddenly, she wasn't so sure. An abstract shape didn't seem like a very good idea anymore. It seemed too . . . easy. Too simplistic.

I have to come up with another idea, Stephanie urged herself. *Fast. And it has to be a better idea than just a design.*

"John Muir!" Stephanie blurted out. The words surprised even her. "We're building John Muir himself. He was an environmentalist, so it totally fits that we would use recycled materials to make a monument to him. . . ."

"The namesake of our school," Allie finished for her. "That's a fabulous idea, Steph!"

"What are *you* making, Grant?" Darcy asked.

"A robot," Grant admitted. "Our sculpture will be called Into the Next Century. But now, I've got to go—the library calls."

"His idea is so lame," Darcy muttered to Stephanie and Allie.

Stephanie smiled. Darcy was right. A sculpture of John Muir was a much better idea. Now the only question was—how in the world were they going to build it?

"Let's work in the kitchen," Stephanie said, coming in her front door. It was late that afternoon.

After the Challenge Day meeting ended and their team's materials were stacked neatly in their work space, Stephanie, Darcy, and Allie took the bus to Stephanie's house to work on their Egypt report.

"Why aren't we working in your room like we always do?" Allie asked. "Don't we need the computer that's there?"

"I can type everything up later. For now I want to give Michelle her space," Stephanie explained. "Since she's feeling so crowded by me."

"Oh, yeah. The letter," Darcy recalled.

Stephanie went up the stairs to get her books on Egypt. They were gone. But she knew she'd left them at the top of the stairs. "Hey! Where'd my books go?" she cried out.

"Your dad probably moved them," Allie called up to her. "You know how neat he is. He's always straightening up."

Stephanie nodded. "You're right. He probably put them in my room."

She peeked inside and saw that Michelle wasn't there. *Good. I won't be crowding her if I slip in to find my books*, Stephanie thought.

She checked around her dresser, under her

bed, even in her closet. No books. Stephanie's heart sped up. Where could they be? *Don't panic,* she told herself. *They've got to be here somewhere.* She headed back downstairs.

"Any luck?" Darcy asked.

Before Stephanie could answer, Michelle, Mandy, and Cassie came in from the kitchen. Each had a cookie in her hand.

"Michelle, have you seen my books on Egypt?" Stephanie asked. "They were up on the stairs yesterday."

Michelle smiled at her. "Good news," she said. "They were due yesterday so I took them back to the library for you."

"You returned them!" Stephanie cried.

Michelle nodded.

"You're kidding, right? This is a joke?" Stephanie asked frantically.

Michelle shook her head. "No."

"Come on," Darcy said, heading for the door. "We have to get to the library fast. I bet we can still get them back."

"Don't bother, you guys," Michelle said. "The books aren't there."

"What?" Stephanie shrieked.

"One of your friends took them all. He was in line ahead of us at the library, and he said he wanted them."

Stephanie felt herself calm down. *A friend has the books,* she thought. *Whew. That means we can definitely get them back.* "Who has the books, Michelle?" she asked.

"Wait. Give me a second and I'll remember his name," Michelle replied. "He has red hair, and he's on the basketball team. . . ."

Stephanie drew in a long breath. No. This wasn't happening. It couldn't be. "Grant?" Stephanie asked.

"That's it," Michelle said. "Grant."

"Nooooo!" Stephanie wailed. She threw herself onto the couch. There was only one Grant she knew. It had to be Grant Munsen.

How could Michelle do this? Stephanie thought. *How could she have given all my research books away to my very worst enemy?*

Chapter
5

Uh-oh, Michelle thought. *This isn't the reaction I expected. Where's the thank-you? Where's the big you're-the-best-Michelle hug?*

"Michelle, how could you do that?" Stephanie demanded. "I needed those books. And you handed them over to Grant Munsen."

"They were overdue," Michelle repeated. "Did you know that?"

"Yes, I knew," Stephanie cried. "I was willing to pay the fine just to have them a while longer. Do you know how many kids in my class would give anything to have those books?"

"No," Michelle replied quietly.

"Even the local bookstores are sold out of books on Egypt," Stephanie went on. "Our entire grade is studying Egypt and everyone has a project due on Egypt by the end of the grading period."

I have to make Stephanie understand, Michelle thought. "I just figured they were due and—"

"Why couldn't you just leave them where I put them and mind your own business?" Stephanie cut her off.

Allie and Darcy stood there staring accusingly at Michelle.

Mandy and Cassie just looked shocked at Stephanie's outburst.

Michelle wished she could disappear. Now Stephanie would *really* want nothing more to do with her. What would she write in her next letter to *Daisy?* Michelle could only imagine.

Dear Libby,
Remember my horrible sister? Well, she gets worse every day. She just ruined my

class report. All the books I needed are gone now, thanks to her. I think she's out to get me. She's gone from bad to worse. What will she do next?

A car horn sounded outside, breaking Michelle out of her thoughts.

"That might be my mother," Mandy said. She hurried to the front door and looked out. "Yup. It's her," she reported. "Come on, Cassie. We have to go."

"We never finished the video," Cassie complained.

"Tell me about it," Mandy grumbled as she pulled on her jacket.

"Sorry, guys," Michelle said. "I just needed to . . ."

"We know, you had to return library books that Stephanie still needs," Mandy said, rolling her eyes.

"We'll call you later, okay?" Cassie said. She followed Mandy out the door.

Michelle's shoulders slumped forward miserably. Stephanie was furious with her. Her friends were definitely not happy. How had this day turned into such a mess?

"What do you want to do now?" Darcy asked Stephanie.

Stephanie shrugged her shoulders in despair. "I have no idea. Let's go to the kitchen and get some ice cream. It might cheer us up, though I doubt anything could make me feel better right now."

Michelle watched them walk into the kitchen, leaving her standing all alone in the middle of the living room.

She felt horrible, but there had to be a way to fix this mess.

If only that kid Grant hadn't taken the books.

Hmm. Why couldn't Stephanie just call Grant and ask for the books back? Michelle wondered. Maybe she was shy about it. Or she didn't really know Grant well enough to ask.

But Grant seemed like a nice guy. Michelle had liked him.

If she could explain the situation to him,

maybe he'd understand. How could she contact him, though? She didn't know his phone number or where he lived.

Then it hit her. The computer! Stephanie's school directory listed everyone's name and e-mail address.

Michelle bolted up the stairs and into her room. She found the directory on Stephanie's dresser. Now, what did Stephanie say Grant's last name was? Something with an *M*.

Aha! She found it. Munsen. Grant Munsen. His online name was Munsenman.

Michelle had to chuckle. *Munsenman?* she thought. *That's pretty funny.* She sat down in front of Stephanie's computer. She could e-mail Grant. But maybe if she was lucky, he was online right now and she could send him an instant message. It was worth a try.

Hi, Grant, Michelle typed into the instant message box. *This is . . .*

She stopped. Should she say she was herself, Michelle? Or would it be better if she pretended to be Stephanie?

Grant might think it was weird that Stephanie had her little sister asking for her books back. It might make Stephanie seem kind of— babyish. It was probably easier to say she was Stephanie.

This is Stephanie, she typed. *How are you?*

She hit Send, then sat back, studying the screen. Would he get the message?

A soft bell sounded. "Yes!" she cheered. He was answering.

I'm the same as I was earlier today, he wrote. *How are you?*

Michelle didn't understand. Earlier today? Then she realized Stephanie must have seen him while she was working on her Challenge Day project. She'd heard Stephanie mention something about it to their dad, so that made sense.

I'm the same, too, Michelle typed in a reply. *Challenge Day sure is fun, isn't it? Even though it's a lot of work.*

You're sure in a better mood, Grant's answer came back.

Michelle wasn't sure what he meant by that. How should she reply? Stephanie had probably been up late the night before, and maybe she'd seemed tired and a little cranky when Grant saw her.

She began to type. *Yes. I feel a lot better now. I didn't get much sleep last night so I wasn't really myself today.*

Oh, he typed back.

Michelle decided this was as good a time as any to get to the point. She started typing. *My sister told me there was a little mix-up today at the library, and that she accidentally gave you my books on Egypt. I still need them for my report. Would you give them back to me?*

There was a long pause. Was Grant thinking about how he wanted to answer? He'd seemed so nice. Michelle couldn't imagine him refusing to give the books back.

Finally the message bell sounded and his words appeared in the IM box. *Admit that my team came up with the recycling idea first and I'll think about it.*

Recycling idea? Now Michelle had *no* idea what Grant was talking about. But whatever it was, it had to be a small price to pay to get those books back. Stephanie was so totally upset about losing them.

Sure. Okay, she wrote back. *You thought of it first.*

Great, he replied. *You can have your books back Monday at school.*

Thanks so much!!! Michelle wrote back. *Bye.*

She turned off the Internet program and shut down the computer. Excellent. She'd saved the day. Wait until Stephanie heard the great news.

Michelle hurried down the stairs and burst into the kitchen.

"Calm down, Steph," Allie was saying. "It was just a big mix-up."

Stephanie paced around the kitchen. She noticed Michelle, but looked away, ignoring her.

Empty bowls sat on the table. It seemed that even ice cream hadn't been enough to cheer Stephanie up this time. Wait until she heard the great news.

Michelle opened her mouth to speak. But Stephanie spoke first.

"How can I calm down? This is a total disaster. I can't believe that Grant Munsen—my
worst enemy—has all our Egypt books."

Michelle's eyed widened. Wait a minute.
Grant Munsen was Stephanie's worst enemy?
Why hadn't someone told her that before?

"Arrrrrgh!" Stephanie clenched her fists
and gave out a growl of frustration. "This is
just like Challenge Day. *I* came up with the
recycling idea first and now he's trying to
claim all the credit for it."

Michelle drew in a long, nervous breath.
Oh, no! She'd just told Grant that *he* could
have credit for the recycling idea.

What had she done now?

Chapter
6

Do either of you have any more quarters?" Stephanie asked Allie and Darcy.

They were in the school library that Monday. All the books on Egypt were already checked out. Stephanie wasn't surprised.

So she, Darcy, and Allie sat together at a long table looking through the thick reference books that had to stay in the library.

"I put every quarter I had in the copy machine," Darcy said. She nodded toward the pages of information they'd already copied. "Don't you think that's enough?"

"Not really," Stephanie said. She sighed. "I can't believe we had everything we needed. And Michelle gave the books away . . . to Grant Munsen!"

Darcy looked up from the notes she was taking. "Michelle didn't give them to Grant to be mean, Steph. She just goofed."

"I hope so," Stephanie said, her mind flashing back to the letter in *Daisy*. "I'd hate to think she was *that* mad at me."

"I saw her face yesterday," Allie said. "She looked pretty shocked that you were upset. I think she expected you to thank her."

"Maybe," Stephanie admitted. "To tell you the truth, I feel pretty bad about blowing up at her. It's just that Grant got me so riled up at the Challenge Day meeting. . . ." She paused. "It wasn't very fair of me, was it? Michelle probably thinks I'm a double pain now. I'll have to find a way to make it up to her."

"Just explain everything. She'll understand," Allie assured her.

Stephanie nodded. "Meanwhile, if none of

us has quarters, I have to copy down this whole long article on the tombs of the fifty sons of Ramses the Second *by hand*," she said.

She stared down at the heavy reference book. The same subject had been covered in one of her books. She clearly remembered reading it.

If only she had it now. If the books were still hers, she wouldn't have to sit here wasting time and getting writer's cramp.

Stephanie suddenly stood up. "This is ridiculous. I'm getting those books back from Grant. He shouldn't have them in the first place and he knows it," she declared.

"He checked them out. They're his," Allie reminded her.

"Finders keepers, you know," Darcy added.

"I don't care," Stephanie insisted. "Michelle returned them without my permission. That means they should never have been returned. Which means Grant shouldn't have gotten them in the first place and, therefore, he has no right to them."

"Are you going to say all that to Grant?" Allie asked.

"Absolutely," Stephanie said.

Darcy turned to Allie. "I think we're in for another battle. King Kong versus Godzilla. Want to watch?"

"No, thanks," Allie declined. "I don't want to be anywhere near it. In fact, I'm going to hide under this library table, where it's safe."

"Very funny," Stephanie said as she gathered her pen and notebook together. "I'm not going to fight with him, I'll just simply and logically *demand* my books back."

"Good lu-uck," Darcy sang out in a doubtful voice.

Stephanie headed into the hall. She checked the clock on the wall. In another few minutes she'd have to get to social studies class. Grant's locker wasn't far from where she was. With luck, she'd have her books before social studies began.

Just be firm and tell him you have to have those books back, she coached herself.

When she was halfway down the hall, she

spotted him opening his locker. *Don't chicken out now,* she thought. *Those books are yours and you're entitled to them.*

Grant noticed her when she was about five lockers away. He looked up and smiled.

Stephanie slowed her pace. Was Grant smiling? At *her?* Why? What was he up to?

He reached into his locker and pulled out a stack of books.

Stephanie stared at them. They were her books. Definitely.

"Got your books," he said.

"I know," Stephanie said. "And I'm here to—"

"Here you go." Grant held the stack out to her.

Stephanie blinked hard. "You're . . . you're *giving* them back to me?" she questioned.

"Of course I am," he replied.

Was this a joke? Stephanie wondered. A trick?

He piled the books into her arms. "Take them. They're yours."

"H—how— Thank you," she cried. "Wow! Really, thanks a lot!"

She felt so relieved. If she hadn't been holding all those books, she might actually have hugged him.

Then she remembered—this was still Grant Munsen—even if he was acting as though space aliens had taken over his body.

Grant grinned. "You didn't expect me to give them back, did you?" he said.

"Not exactly," she agreed.

He shut his locker and leaned against it. "Listen, Stephanie, I should apologize for the way I've been acting. I used to think you were nothing but snooty and uptight."

"But I'm not," Stephanie insisted.

"I know that now," Grant agreed. "After Saturday I realized there's another side to you."

Saturday?

Mentally, Stephanie ran through the events of Saturday. As far as she could remember she and Grant hadn't exchanged a single friendly word. What had happened on Saturday to change his mind about her?

Then it came to her. On Saturday Grant finally

saw that she couldn't be pushed around. He'd gained a whole new respect for her. Stephanie liked that idea—and it made her like Grant.

Just a little, though.

"After this I hope we can cooperate more," Grant went on. "We'll still be on different teams, but I hope we can be *friendly* rivals."

Stephanie smiled at him. "Me, too," she agreed.

"Great," he said, grinning back at her.

What an adorable smile, she observed.

Wait a minute—where had that thought come from?

The bell rang and the hallway began to fill with people. "I've got to get going," Stephanie said. "Thanks again for the books."

"No problem," Grant replied. With a wave, he headed off down the hall.

Stephanie watched him leave. What was happening here? What was with Grant's total change in attitude?

An idea struck her: Did Grant suddenly like her? Did he like her as more than just a friend?

She turned and headed toward social studies, feeling a smile creep across her face. She wondered if this could be the beginning of something new between her and Grant—something a lot more interesting than a rivalry.

Michelle

Chapter
7

Michelle chewed on her peanut butter sandwich and tried to follow the conversation at her lunch table that Monday.

Cassie and Mandy were talking to two other girls in their class, Karlee and Anna. "Wasn't it funny when Anna's ball kept getting stuck in the reset machine? That poor guy had to come get it unstuck every few minutes," Mandy said with a laugh.

"Yeah, but the most hysterical part was when my ball went into the other lane." Karlee giggled. "I wanted to run away and hide."

Michelle was totally confused. Reset machines? Lanes? What was everyone talking about?

"And then," Cassie said with a giggle, "do you remember when the guy next to us turned and said—"

"Wait a minute," Michelle interrupted. "Did I miss something?"

Cassie and Mandy glanced at each other. Michelle thought they looked guilty.

"What?" she prodded them to explain. "What's going on?"

"You *did* miss something, I guess," Mandy answered. "The four of us went bowling and had pizza yesterday."

"Without me?" Michelle cried.

She couldn't believe it. Cassie and Mandy had never done something fun without her before.

"Why didn't you call me?" Michelle demanded to know.

"Well . . ." Cassie began. "You see . . ."

"See you guys later," Anna said. She and Karlee got up from the table.

"Yeah. See ya," Cassie told them with a smile and a wave.

"I'm sorry, Michelle," Mandy jumped in when they were gone. "But we didn't call you because we didn't want to have another day like Saturday."

"Saturday wasn't my fault," Michelle protested.

"Yes, it was," Mandy argued. "On Friday, you didn't want to hang out because you were upset about Stephanie. On Saturday, you ignored us because you were thinking about Stephanie."

"Well, it's been worrying me," Michelle insisted.

"I know, but then you dragged us all the way to the library when Stephanie didn't even want you to return her books in the first place," Mandy said. "We didn't get to spend a special friend day together. We didn't even get to finish the video. The entire day was a waste!"

"It's true, Michelle," Cassie put in. "You haven't been much fun lately."

Michelle knew her friends were making

good points. She *had* been thinking only about Stephanie lately. And she had been ignoring her friends. "I'm sorry, guys," she apologized.

"We're not mad at you, Michelle," Cassie said.

"We just figured you were too busy for us," Mandy told her.

"How about giving me a second chance?" Michelle asked. "I really, really do want to do something fun with you guys. After all, you are my best friends."

"Okay. If you promise that you won't even think about Stephanie while you're with us," Mandy agreed.

"I promise," Michelle said eagerly.

"Great. Then let's plan something. What should we do?" Mandy asked.

"Let's have a best-friends-only pizza party tomorrow after school," Michelle suggested.

"It's a deal," Mandy said.

Cassie turned to Mandy. "Since she's not allowed to think about Stephanie tomorrow, could I ask Michelle one question about her right now? It's a small one."

Mandy sighed. "If you have to."

"Did Stephanie forgive you for returning her books?" Cassie asked.

"The whole thing is even worse than it was before," Michelle told her. She explained the whole e-mail fiasco. Including the part about the Challenge event idea.

"If Stephanie finds out what I did, she'll really want to kill me," Michelle wailed.

"Uh-oh," Mandy said. "What are you going to do?"

"I don't know. Hope Grant never mentions it?" Michelle replied.

"He'll mention it," Mandy said.

Michelle slumped down in her seat.

"Wait. I think I have an idea," Cassie said. "Why don't you write Grant another e-mail saying that you're Stephanie and you were only kidding? That the idea was yours first."

"Hey, that might work," Michelle agreed. "When I get home I'll send him an e-mail or an Instant Message right away."

"Why wait till later?" Mandy asked. "We can go to the computer room and do it right now. It's open at lunchtime for anyone who wants to use it."

"You're right," Michelle cried, jumping up from her seat. "Let's go."

The three friends walked as fast as they could down the hall to the computer room.

Mr. Pelligrino, the computer teacher, was at his desk grading papers. "We're just sending an e-mail, okay?" Michelle checked in as she passed him.

"Need help?" he asked.

"No, thanks," she replied.

Michelle slid into a chair in front of a computer. Cassie and Mandy pulled up seats alongside hers. Michelle turned on the computer, logged on to the Internet and hit the Write button.

Grant was in school, so there was no sense trying to send him an instant message. She'd have to write an e-mail.

She began to type. *Hi, Grant. It's me, Stephanie. Did you really think I agreed that the recycling idea was yours? No way! Recycling was my idea and you know it. Everyone knows it.* She looked up at Mandy. "Enough?" she checked.

"I know! Tell him Stephanie said the idea was his only so he'd give her the books back," Mandy suggested.

"But if I write that he *won't* give her back the books," Michelle worried.

"He won't get this message until after school," Mandy reminded her. "By then he'll have returned the books."

Michelle sighed. "I don't know . . ."

"If he's Stephanie's worst enemy, then he must have done something pretty bad to her," Cassie pointed out.

"That's true," Michelle agreed. She remembered how angry Stephanie had been at Grant. Then she went back to her message. *The only reason I agreed that the idea was yours was to get those books back. Faked you out, didn't I?*

"Perfect," Mandy declared.

"You really think so?" Michelle asked uncertainly.

"Definitely," Cassie told her.

"Once you tell her what you've done, Stephanie will think you're the greatest sister alive," Mandy cheered.

"Okay," Michelle said. She hit the Send button.

Soon Grant would read the e-mail and everything would be back the way Stephanie wanted it. Then Stephanie would absolutely, positively like Michelle again.

Wouldn't she?

Stephanie

Chapter
8

"That's an awesome idea, Grant," Stephanie said that afternoon after school. "Thanks!"

Everyone was in the gym for a scheduled Challenge Day meeting. Each team was now busily creating their works of art.

Grant had just suggested that his team and Stephanie's team pool all of their recycled materials. He'd already moved his pile of things next to Stephanie's.

They agreed that Grant's group would use only bottles and cans on their sculpture, while

Stephanie's team would use boxes and paper. "Anything in between is up for grabs," Grant added.

"That seems fair," Stephanie agreed. She smiled at him. "Working together is much better, isn't it?" she asked.

"Absolutely," he agreed. His gray eyes sparkled in a way she'd never noticed before. It made him absolutely adorable.

A mischievous grin came over his face. "Now let's see your team try to beat Century Man the robot!"

"No problem." Stephanie took the challenge. "You're on."

Stephanie joined her team and explained the new deal with Grant. "Let's go see what we can come up with," she directed them.

The group headed over to the pile of shared materials to collect supplies.

"That little talk looked pretty friendly," Darcy teased as she walked to the pile with Stephanie. "What's going on?"

"Nothing," Stephanie insisted. Still, she felt her face grow warm.

"You're blushing," Darcy said with a giggle. "Something *is* going on."

"It's just that Grant's been so much nicer lately," Stephanie said. "He's always acted like such a jerk. I never knew he had this nice side to him. I have to admit, I really like it."

"He never saw the nice side of you, either," Allie pointed out.

"I guess that's true," Stephanie told her.

They joined the others at the pile. Everyone on Grant's team was also picking through the materials. They chose only cans and bottles, just as she and Grant had agreed.

Stephanie's team took paper and boxes. They also collected hangers, telephone wire, and various other odds and ends.

When they got back to their spot, Stephanie explained her plan. Sitting cross-legged, she laid out the pictures of John Muir that she had printed from her computer research.

"Here's what he really looked like," she said. "We won't be able to make him look exactly real, but we can make a sort-of likeness." Then she showed her team Allie's revised sketch—an abstract representation of John Muir.

"I was thinking we could build his frame from wire and other stuff. Then we could use the boxes and paper to make papier-mâché clothing for him. Allie can draw his face. That way, everyone will know who he is."

"That's cool," Ezra said. "I like it."

The others agreed. They set to work building their sculpture's torso and legs.

Allie and Stephanie sat on the floor, twisting telephone wire into the shape of two feet. "We can give him shoe-box shoes," Allie suggested.

As they worked, Grant wandered over. "No spying," Stephanie teased.

"I'm not spying," he replied with a smile. "I just thought I'd say hi."

Stephanie glanced over at his project. "Century Man is getting pretty big," she noted.

"Yep. How big is Mr. Muir going to be?"

"None of your business," she answered.

Although their words were competitive, their voices were friendly.

Yeah, Stephanie thought. *This is so much better.*

"Oh, I also just wanted to say . . . Century Man rules!" Grant punched a fist into the air as he walked away.

"Did you say *drools?*" Stephanie asked.

He laughed and rejoined his team.

"Stephanie, you *like* him," Allie whispered.

"I do not," Stephanie argued.

"Please, don't even try to fool us. It shows." Darcy nudged Stephanie with her elbow. "I think he likes you, too."

"Really?" Stephanie asked, pleased. "I guess he *is* sort of interesting."

"And cute," Allie added.

Stephanie sneaked a peek at Grant. She had to admit it—he was cute.

That evening Stephanie, Darcy, and Allie gathered in Stephanie's bedroom to work on their Egypt report.

They had until the end of the semester to complete the report, but why not hand it in early? Stephanie figured.

"This will be a breeze now that we have the books back," Stephanie assured her friends.

"I can't believe Grant just handed them over. Boy, were we ever wrong about him," Darcy said.

"That's for sure," Allie agreed.

"So listen, guys. The other night—before I knew I'd have these books back—I was doing research on the Internet," Stephanie said, turning on the computer. "I found a great map. I thought I could print it out and glue it to the report cover."

"Good idea," Allie said.

Stephanie logged on to the Internet. *"You have mail"* the electronic computer voice told her.

She hit the Read icon. "It's from Munsenman," she told her friends excitedly.

"How cool! He's e-mailing you at home now," Allie squeaked. "What does he say? What does he say?"

Darcy and Allie stood behind Stephanie. She opened up his mail and read:

It looks like I was right about you all along. What a bummer. You're just as self-centered, conceited, and full of yourself as I always thought. I can't believe you pretended to be nice just to get the books. It just shows who you really are.

We'll see who laughs last when Century Man blows your rickety old geezer out of the water.

Grant

Stephanie's jaw dropped in horrified disbelief. What was Grant talking about?

She looked at her friends. They wore similar expressions of dumbfounded amazement.

"You have to write him back," Allie murmured, still staring at Grant's e-mail. "Something's gone totally wrong here."

Stephanie closed the letter. She couldn't stand to look at it another second. What had given Grant the idea that she had tricked him?

"Somebody said something to him," Stephanie guessed. "That has to be the answer.

They must have told him I was being nice just to get the books back."

"But who even knew about the books?" Darcy asked.

"And who would lie about me like that?" Stephanie added. "Who would do something *so mean?*"

"Hi, everybody," Michelle greeted them cheerfully as she walked in the door. She glanced at the Egypt books sitting on the desk. "All right! You got them back!" she cried, clapping her hands.

"Yes. Grant gave them back to me," Stephanie told her.

"Great! Then my plan worked," Michelle cried.

Stephanie stared at her sister. "Plan? What plan? Did you have something to do with Grant giving me my books back?"

Michelle beamed. "I didn't want to tell you, because I didn't want you to be mad, but I e-mailed Grant, pretending to be you and asked for them back."

"Okay. So you didn't tell me because . . .

because you thought I'd be mad that you pretended to be me?" Stephanie asked slowly. She wasn't sure she understood.

"Not exactly," Michelle answered. "I thought you'd be mad because in order to get the books back I had to do something."

"What?" Stephanie asked suspiciously.

"I had to tell Grant that he came up with the recycling idea first."

"Michelle!" Stephanie cried. "You didn't!"

It all made sense now. No wonder Grant had been so friendly. He thought he had won—that Stephanie had admitted defeat.

"Don't get upset," Michelle said quickly. "I fixed it all this afternoon. I wrote Grant another e-mail saying that it was all just a trick."

Stephanie felt a knot forming in the pit of her stomach. She didn't like the sound of this.

"I told him you said the recycling idea was his only to get the books back," Michelle continued. "And that you didn't believe he had the idea first for a minute. It was great! I got your books back for you, and I let Grant know exactly how you feel about him. Aren't you happy?"

Michelle

Chapter
9

Michelle stood there, smiling. Waiting for the cheering to start. Ready to get a high-five from her big sister.

Instead, Stephanie's face grew red.

"What?" Michelle asked, not understanding. "Is something wrong?"

"Michelle," Stephanie said quietly, "are you on some kind of mission to destroy my life?"

"What do you mean?" Michelle asked.

"Grant and I were getting along so well. Now you've ruined everything!" Stephanie cried. "He totally despises me. He thinks I'm the lowest of the low."

"But I thought he was your worst enemy," Michelle reminded her. "You said that to Darcy and Allie yesterday."

Michelle's head felt as if it were spinning. How could things have changed so much in just one day?

"Michelle, I don't know why you hate me so much, but you have to stop messing me up all the time. It's driving me crazy!" Stephanie jumped up from her chair and stalked out of the room.

"Stephanie," Darcy called. "Wait!" She and Allie gathered their things and followed her out.

Michelle opened her mouth but no words came. She couldn't remember a time when Stephanie had been this angry at her.

But, wait a minute, Stephanie had no reason to be angry! Michelle realized. She was only trying to help her sister, and no matter what she did, it seemed that all Stephanie did was yell at her.

She lay down on her bed and folded her arms. She stared at the ceiling.

Who did Stephanie think she was, anyway? She hadn't even given Michelle a chance to explain.

What a disaster the last few days had been. All Michelle had done was drive herself crazy by trying to be nice to Stephanie.

And did Stephanie thank her for it?

Was she even the tiniest bit grateful?

No!

Ever since that letter in *Daisy*, nothing had been the same. Michelle wished she'd never read it. Or Libby's answer, either.

"Be nice," Libby wrote. As if it were that simple. How could you be nice to someone who was totally mean to you? Michelle decided she was never going to read Libby's column again.

A soft computer bell rang. Michelle sat up. A gray box had come on to the middle of the screen.

Crawling to the end of the bed, she read it. *Do you want to stay online?* asked the writing on the screen.

Michelle scooted over to the computer and hit *yes*. The sound had reminded her of something.

Monday through Friday evenings Libby held an online chat at the *Daisy* Web site. It would be the perfect chance to tell Miss Know-It-All exactly what she thought of her stupid advice.

Michelle got to the Web site. Pictures of smiling girls in stylish clothing having fun were everywhere. Big, colorful daisies bordered the screen.

Looks like one big party, she thought angrily as she found her way into the chat room.

The picture of a cheerful, dark-haired young woman appeared on the screen. Her name was written under her picture. Libby Greenfield, Ph.D.

Michelle read the chat that appeared on the screen. Libby was talking to a girl about how to overcome shyness. When it seemed she was done, Michelle jumped in.

"In this month's issue of Daisy *you gave some really crummy advice,"* she began. She went on to tell how her sister had written in complain-

ing about her, and how Libby had advised her to be extra nice.

Libby typed in her response. *"I remember the letter. The advice was meant for your sister, not you. Did she follow it?"*

"No," Michelle typed. *"But I did."* She continued on, explaining how she'd tried so hard to be the best sister in the world—and how it had all backfired. *Now my sister is angrier at me than ever*, she finished.

There was a brief pause, then Libby got back to her. *"There is such a thing as being too nice. It sounds to me like your sister is taking advantage of you. Don't let her. I recall that I also advised letting her have more space. I think you should stop trying to win her over.*

"A relationship is a two-way street," Libby continued. *"You two are obviously both having trouble dealing with each other. My advice is to stay as far apart as you can. Then, after time has passed and you both have calmed down, you'll be able to discuss your differences."*

Michelle thought that sounded reasonable. Maybe Libby wasn't that off base, after all.

"Thanks. I'll try it," Michelle typed. Then she left the chat, closed the Web site, and logged off the Internet.

Looking around the bedroom, she thought about Libby's advice. How could she possibly create space between Stephanie and herself? They not only lived in the same house, they slept in the same bedroom.

"I'll just have to *make* the space," she said out loud as she got up from her chair.

At the bottom of the clothes closet, she found her shoe box filled with art supplies. In it was a roll of masking tape.

She attached one end of the tape to the middle of the table that stood between their twin beds. She set a heavy paperweight on top of it.

She dragged the tape down the front of the table and along the floor. She continued over the middle of the computer desk and all the way to the very end of the room.

There! The room was divided in half. *I'll stay on my half and Stephanie can stay on hers,* she thought. *From now on, if Stephanie didn't want to share space with her, she wouldn't have to!*

Stephanie

Chapter 10

What in the world is this? Stephanie thought. She gazed at the masking-tape line down the middle of her bedroom.

She had just come back upstairs after Darcy and Allie left. Together, after Stephanie had calmed down, they'd roughed out the entire report on Egypt, working in the kitchen. Now all Stephanie had to do was type it on her computer.

But now there was another problem to deal with: whatever Michelle meant by this line of tape.

Stephanie felt a strange emptiness in the pit

of her stomach. The letter in *Daisy* had been only the tip of the iceberg—her first clue about how Michelle really felt. But now it seemed that Michelle disliked her so much, she was actually going out of her way to be mean.

Michelle lay on her bed, reading a book. She didn't look up when Stephanie entered.

"Michelle, what's this?" Stephanie asked wearily.

"What does it look like?" Michelle asked from behind her book.

Stephanie sat on her bed, across from Michelle. "It looks like you've divided the room in half."

"Exactly right," Michelle answered. "From now on we're going to pretend there's a wall down the middle of this room. You stay on your side. I'll stay on mine. That way, we'll both have our own space."

"Sorry, Michelle, but there are a few problems with your plan," Stephanie told her.

"Like what?" Michelle asked, putting down her book.

"Are you planning to pole-vault over to

your side of the room?" Stephanie asked. "You must be, because otherwise I don't see how you're going to get there—since the door is on my side of the tape."

"Oh, very funny." Michelle said. "Well, in that case, you're going to have a few problems, too. You won't be able to get to the clothes closet. I guess you'll be able to wear only the clothes in your dresser."

"And you'll be stuck without any CDs since the CD stand is on my side of the room," Stephanie reminded her.

"That's fine with me," Michelle replied. "I'll get new CDs."

Stephanie rested her forehead in her hand. She couldn't believe she was really having this conversation with Michelle. "I don't have time for this," she said, heading for the computer. "I have a big report to write."

Michelle rolled off her bed and stood in front of the computer. "Uh-uh. It's on my side of the room," she insisted.

"The tape goes down the middle of table," Stephanie told her.

"But the *computer* is on my side," Michelle said.

This was too much. Stephanie felt herself losing patience. "Michelle, get out of my way," she spoke firmly.

Michelle folded her arms stubbornly.

"Mich-e-lle," Stephanie growled through clenched teeth. "I'm warning you. Move!"

Michelle shook her head.

"I'm not kidding!" Stephanie yelled. "I have to do this report. Now let me use the computer." She yanked the chair out from the desk and threw herself into it. Michelle stood where she was, still glaring angrily at Stephanie.

"Would you go away?" Stephanie asked irritably. "I can't write with you staring at the back of my head."

Stephanie turned on the computer. She could hear Michelle returning to her bed.

For a moment she thought about writing to Grant. But she could still feel Michelle staring at her. Quickly, she checked over her left shoulder.

Michelle's eyes peered over the top of her book.

"Stop looking at me!" Stephanie demanded. She opened the word processing program and began typing up the notes she and her friends had made.

An hour later she was nearing the end of the report. She stopped to stretch and roll her neck. *I still need to print out that map of Egypt,* she remembered.

As she waited for the Internet connection to load up, she checked over her shoulder to see if Michelle had fallen asleep. Her sister wasn't in her bed. *I didn't even hear her leave,* Stephanie realized.

As the Internet came on, she remembered that Grant's angry letter was still sitting in the mail file. She pulled it up and read it again.

What a mess. How would she ever fix this?

And how would she ever make things right with Michelle again?

Stephanie

Chapter 11

Stephanie groggily opened her eyes and peered at the clock. It was only six-thirty in the morning. Why was she awake?

Michelle passed in front of Stephanie's bed, getting ready for school.

Wham! She threw her sneakers down to the floor.

Slam! She closed the closet door with a bang.

Stephanie squeezed her eyes shut. Michelle's racket was the reason she was awake. No doubt about it. "Please stop doing that," Stephanie requested through gritted teeth.

Michelle glared at her, but didn't say anything. She left the room, shutting the door loudly behind her.

Fine, Stephanie thought angrily. *Don't speak to me. I don't care.*

She knew that wasn't true, though. She didn't like fighting with Michelle. It made her feel so sad inside.

It also made her confused. What did Michelle have to be angry about, anyway? Why had she written that letter to *Daisy* in the first place?

I can't think about Michelle now, Stephanie decided. There were other, more distressing things to worry about.

Like Grant. The thought of facing him that day in school made her stomach twist into a knot.

When she arrived at school, she went directly to his locker. He wasn't there. She waited nearly five minutes before giving in and reporting to homeroom.

At lunch Grant sat with a big group of his friends. Most of them were from the varsity basketball team.

"I can't just walk over there," Stephanie told Allie. "I feel too funny."

"I would, too," Allie agreed. "Why don't you wait until after school? When we work on Challenge Day in the gym you can find some time to talk with him alone."

"Good idea," Stephanie said.

But the moment she walked into the gym at the end of the day, there was a problem. Ezra hurried over to her. "Grant's team went back on our deal," he said. "Look! They're using paper and boxes. Grant told them to."

Stephanie stared across the gym. Ezra was right. Century Man was being fitted with a large box belly and chest.

Jessica jogged over. "You're the team captain, Stephanie. You have to say something."

Stephanie nodded. "Okay. I'll deal with it." She sighed. This wasn't the way she wanted to start off a conversation with Grant—by arguing.

But as team captain, it was her job. She had no choice.

"Hi, Grant," she greeted him when she got

across the gym. "What's happening here? I thought we made a deal about dividing the materials."

He looked at her and his face hardened. "Oh, did you believe that? Oh, no. That was just a trick. We didn't want you to use any of the bottles and cans. Now that we've got them all, we don't care about you anymore."

"Grant, that isn't fair," Stephanie protested.

"Who cares about fairness?" he replied. "Certainly not you."

"Listen, we have to talk," Stephanie said.

"I'm done talking to you," he said, then turned his back.

"But, you don't understand!" she insisted.

He helped his teammate hold up one of the boxes while the others used silver duct tape to seal it into position. Stephanie stood there a moment longer. Finally she realized that Grant wasn't going to turn around—not as long as she was there.

She walked back to her group. "The deal is totally off," she told them. "You can use any bottles and cans you find."

"There are none left," Darcy pointed out. "They took them all yesterday."

"Look, forget about Grant's team," Stephanie said. "Let's just get to work."

Their sculpture's legs, arms, hands, feet, and torso had been shaped. They had formed them from wire, foil, ribbon, and old wire screens. Now they needed to put it all together.

"My idea is that we use what's left of the telephone wire to stitch it all together," she told them. "Then after that, I think we'd better break into groups. One group has to make his head. Other groups can get started on his clothing."

Putting the pieces together wasn't as easy as she'd hoped. The telephone wire stretched sometimes. The sculpture's arms and legs dangled loosely.

The sculpture was nearly five feet tall without its head. *Which would be pretty impressive,* Stephanie thought. *If it didn't fall over like a floppy marionette.*

She glanced over at Century Man. He stood

straight up, nearly six feet tall. His aluminum-can arms and legs were sturdy. Grant's team was making the statue's head from a box.

"They're going to win," Ezra pronounced, gazing in the same direction.

"Don't say that," Stephanie told him. But there was no getting away from it. It looked as if Grant were right after all. Her Challenge project was going to lose—big time.

Which was no surprise, because lately, it seemed as if Stephanie couldn't win at anything.

Later that afternoon Stephanie stood in the living room, talking to Darcy on the phone. "Yeah, I think our Egypt report looks pretty good," she said.

Allie, Darcy, and Stephanie planned to meet at Darcy's house. Together they would read over the Egypt report Stephanie had typed up.

"Allie's mother is going to pick me up any minute so I'll see you soon," Stephanie said.

Outside, a car horn honked. It had to be Allie and her mother. Perfect timing!

Stephanie hung up and grabbed her hooded sweatshirt from the couch. She headed for the front door. As she pulled it open, the phone rang.

"Hello?" Stephanie answered.

"Hi, it's Mandy. Is Michelle there?"

"Michelle!" Stephanie shouted loudly. No answer.

She shouted again. "Michelle!"

Danny popped his head out from the kitchen door. "Michelle is walking Comet," he told her. "She'll be right back."

"She'll be right back," Stephanie told Mandy.

"Could you give her a message for me?" Mandy requested.

Stephanie worked to keep impatience out of her voice. She was in a hurry. "Sure," she said. "What is it?"

"We've moved our best-friends celebration from Joe's Pizzeria to Mario's Pizza Palace. Tell her we'll meet her there in half an hour. Okay?"

"Okay. Bye," Stephanie said, hanging up. She ran out the door to the car.

"Oh, no!" she said as Allie's mother pulled away from the curb.

"What?" Allie asked.

"I forgot to write down a message for Michelle," she explained. "Her friends are meeting someplace other than they originally planned." She bit her lip. "Oh, well, I'll call from Darcy's to let her know."

"I hope we get there before Michelle leaves to meet her friends," Allie said.

"Me, too," Stephanie agreed. "But I'm not worried. After everything Michelle has pulled this week, I don't think forgetting one little message is such a big deal."

Michelle

Chapter
12

"Are we early?" Michelle asked Danny as they stepped into Joe's Pizzeria in the mall. She didn't see Cassie or Mandy anywhere.

Danny checked his watch. "Nope. We're right on time. I guess they're running late. I'll wait here with you until they arrive."

"Dad," Michelle said slowly. "I don't want to make you feel bad or anything, but . . ."

"Sitting here with your dad is too embarrassing?" he guessed.

"I'm not embarrassed by you," Michelle

was quick to explain. "But it does make me seem a little . . . babyish."

"I understand," Danny said with a smile. "Listen. I'll be over at the garden supply place across the way. After that I'm going to that cooking place right next to it. That's where I'll be if you need me. Otherwise I'll come back here in an hour and a half to take you home."

"Okay," Michelle replied. "Thanks."

Michelle found an empty table and slid into it. When the waitress approached, she ordered a soda. "I'm waiting for friends," she explained. "We'll order when they get here."

The waitress brought the soda, put down a menu, and left. Michelle had never sat alone in a public place before. It was a weird feeling. *I wonder if these people think I'm some kind of loser with no friends*, she worried.

The paper place mat had a map of Italy on it. She read all the names of the cities. Unfortunately, that didn't take very long.

Then she started on the menu. Pizza with

cheese. Pizza with pepperoni. Pizza with sausage. Not exactly thrilling reading.

"Where *are* they?" Michelle muttered, closing the menu.

The clock on the wall seemed to be moving slower than normal. Staring at the minute hand almost put Michelle to sleep.

"Excuse me," she asked the passing waitress after a while. "Is that clock working?"

The waitress smiled softly. "Yes, it is. You've been here for fifteen minutes."

"It seems like three hours," Michelle commented.

"Time goes slowly when you're waiting," the waitress said kindly. "Are you sure you have the time and place right?"

"Positive," Michelle answered. But the waitress's words made her wonder. Had she gotten it wrong?

She paid for her soda and left. There was another pizza place on the first floor of the mall. Michelle quickly checked there, but still didn't find her friends.

The escalator back upstairs gave a good

view of the entire mall. Michelle rode it all the way to the third level, then back down. Her friends just weren't anywhere.

Michelle trudged into the cooking store. She found Danny at the check-out counter. "What's the matter, Michelle?" he asked the moment he saw her expression.

"Cassie and Mandy never showed up," she admitted.

"Oh, that's too bad," he sympathized. "Something must have happened. Want to call them on my cell phone?"

Michelle took the phone from him and dialed Cassie's and Mandy's numbers. But answering machines picked up at both places. "No luck," she reported. "I can't believe my two best friends would stand me up like this."

Danny put a hand on her shoulder. "Wait until you find out what happened before you get mad," he advised.

Michelle couldn't help feeling disappointed and angry. Last Sunday her best friends had gone bowling without her. Today they'd probably forgotten all about their pizza date.

How could they when they had made such a stink about having a best-friends day?

The moment she got home, Michelle called Mandy again. This time, Mandy picked up the phone.

"Where were the two of you?" Michelle cried. "I waited and waited. I felt like a total idiot!"

"We were where we said we'd be," Mandy answered.

"No, you weren't. I was at Joe's at four-thirty sharp and I didn't see you anywhere!"

"That's because we were meeting at Mario's Pizza Palace. Didn't you get the message?"

Michelle paused. "Message?"

"I spoke to Stephanie. Didn't she tell you?"

"No," Michelle said. She frowned. Stephanie must have run out of the house without giving her the message.

"Stephanie didn't tell me anything," Michelle apologized. "I'm sorry I yelled at you."

"You should be," Mandy replied.

Michelle heard a click. "Hello?" she asked. No response.

She stared at the receiver. One of her best friends had just hung up on her.

Great, Michelle thought. Now not only was she fighting with her sister, she'd blown her second chance with her two best friends.

Now, Michelle thought, *nobody likes me!*

Chapter
13

Michelle! You knocked my books off the coffee table on purpose!" Stephanie cried.

"I bumped into the coffee table by accident!" Michelle shouted back. "Why would I want to knock over your dumb books?"

Their father appeared at the top of the stairs. "Girls!" he cried. "Stop that—right now!"

Danny's stern expression told Stephanie he meant business. He didn't lose his temper often, but when he did, it was serious.

Danny walked down the stairs to the living room. "I've just about had it with this fight-

108

ing," he told them both. "I walked past your bedroom and saw the masking-tape line running down the middle of it. What is going on with you two?"

"Ask her," Stephanie said, pointing at Michelle.

"Stephanie wants her own room, so I'm letting her have it," Michelle explained.

"No, you're not," Danny differed. "Michelle, I want you to go upstairs and remove that tape this minute."

"All right," Michelle grumbled. She jogged up the stairs.

Danny turned to Stephanie. "Can you tell me why you two are fighting all the time?"

"A few days ago Michelle started acting incredibly weird. It's like she wants to cause trouble for me," Stephanie answered.

"Michelle told me you didn't give her an important message yesterday," he said. "Isn't that causing trouble for her?"

"Well, I meant to give it to her," Stephanie said. "I just forgot. You always say everyone makes mistakes."

"That's true—as long as it really was a mistake."

Stephanie looked down at her sneakers. It hadn't really been a mistake. She could have called from Darcy's house, but she didn't bother.

"If you can't be nice to Michelle, don't go out of your way to fight with her," Danny said firmly. "Understand?"

"Yes," she answered.

"Meanwhile, I want you to think long and hard about what might have started this whole thing in the first place," Danny instructed. "I'm going to ask your sister to do the same thing." He turned and headed for the kitchen.

What had started this? Stephanie asked herself.

She remembered the letter in *Daisy*. But what caused Michelle to write that letter in the first place?

Michelle stomped down the stairs with a huge wad of used masking tape in her hands. She pushed through the swinging door into the kitchen.

When did she go from adoring me to hating me? Stephanie wondered. She tried to think of an incident, something she might have done to turn Michelle against her.

Naturally, they'd had their little fights. All sisters did. But nothing major had happened, nothing to wreck their whole relationship.

That Libby sure didn't help, either, Stephanie thought. *She said to give Michelle space. Well, I tried. It only seemed to make things worse.*

Stephanie remembered that Wednesday was one of the "Dear Libby" chat nights. *I'm going to tell her what I think of her dumb advice,* she decided.

Getting off the couch, she went upstairs to her computer. In minutes she was into the *Daisy* Web site. She connected to the "Dear Libby" chat section.

A note was posted at the top of the page.

The "Dear Libby" chat has been postponed for the evening because of a personal scheduling conflict. Try again on Friday. In the meantime, we have posted a transcript of Libby's most recent Monday chat for your reading pleasure.

Stephanie was about to click out of the chat when a word caught her eye. It was a name—Michelle's screen name.

She'd contacted Libby just last Monday! What did she have to say? Stephanie had to know, so she began to read.

As her eyes scanned the page, they widened in surprise.

Could this be true? Did Michelle really think that she was being nice and Stephanie was being mean?

She sat back in her chair and thought about it.

Returning those library books *might* have been an honest mistake. Michelle didn't know she wasn't finished with them. They *were* late, after all.

And she might not have meant any harm by giving them to Grant, either. He asked for the books. Michelle didn't know Stephanie still needed them. She *also* didn't know that Grant wasn't really her friend.

After that, she'd only been trying to fix what she'd done.

Stephanie clicked out of the *Daisy* Web site. Now she understood a lot. Michelle didn't hate her. She wanted Stephanie to be nicer to her—that's why she'd written the letter to *Daisy* in the first place. That was why she started acting so wacky.

I thought I was nice to her, Stephanie considered. *But I guess I haven't been doing a good enough job. And lately I've been downright mean.*

Stephanie realized she had made a total mess of their friendship. It was time for her to fix it.

Not tonight—she realized Michelle was probably still too mad. But tomorrow Michelle would be in for the surprise of her life.

Michelle

Chapter
14

Michelle sneaked a peek at Mandy and Cassie. She sat across the cafeteria about to eat her sandwich by herself.

She sighed. Her sister and her best friends couldn't stand her. She'd never felt so alone in her life.

This morning she had wanted to talk to Stephanie. She planned to tell her sister she forgave her for not giving her the message. But this morning Stephanie left for school way too early, so their talk would have to wait. *Maybe things will be better by this afternoon,* Michelle told herself.

She glanced toward the door. A pizza delivery person was walking into the cafeteria. Mrs. LoPuzzo, the teacher on lunch duty, spoke to him.

Then she looked over at Mandy and Cassie and called them over with a wave of her hand. She turned toward Michelle, summoning her, too.

What's going on? Michelle wondered as she walked across the cafeteria.

"Girls," Mrs. LoPuzzo said to them. "This man says he has a pizza for the three of you. Did you order it?"

The girls shook their heads.

"I'm sorry," Mrs. LoPuzzo told the delivery person. "Since they can't pay for it, I'll have to—"

"It's paid for," the delivery guy cut her off. "Even the tip."

"It is?" Michelle asked.

The delivery guy nodded. "It's all yours, little lady."

He handed Mrs. LoPuzzo a folded note, which she quickly read.

"Very well, then," Mrs. LoPuzzo agreed. "I guess it's your pizza, girls."

Michelle took the huge box from the delivery man. She looked at Cassie and Mandy, bewildered. From the looks on their faces, Michelle could tell they were just as confused as she was.

"Hey," Mandy shrugged. "It's a free pizza. Let's eat it."

"It sure smells good," Michelle agreed.

Together, they sat at a nearby table. Kids all over the cafeteria craned their necks to get a look at what was going on.

"Who do you think sent this to us?" Cassie wondered.

"I have no idea," Mandy admitted. "Do you, Michelle?"

"Not a clue," Michelle replied honestly. "I hope it's not some kind of gag pizza. You know, the kind with really hot pepper flakes all over it or something."

"No way," Mandy disagreed. "That was a real Mario's pizza guy. He had the official shirt on and everything. Besides, look at the box. This pizza is definitely the real thing."

"We might as well open it," Cassie suggested. She helped Michelle lift the box lid.

"Hey, there's a note in here," Michelle exclaimed. She plucked it from the inside of the box lid. "It's Stephanie's handwriting," she noted.

"What does she say?" Cassie asked.

Michelle read the oil-splotched note. "Dear Michelle, Mandy, and Cassie. I'm sending this pizza to say I'm sorry for messing up your pizza celebration. It was totally my fault. I'm very sorry. Enjoy this pizza. Love, Stephanie."

Michelle put the note down on the table. Her heart felt light with happiness.

Love, Stephanie, the note said. Stephanie loved her! She'd done this nice thing to make up with her. Maybe their fighting was finally over.

She smiled across the pizza at her friends. "I'm glad things are better with Stephanie. Are we friends again, too?"

Cassie nodded, smiling. She began pulling apart slices of pizza and handing them to Mandy and Michelle.

"I've been thinking about it, and I'm really sorry I hung up on you. It wasn't your fault that you didn't get the message yesterday," Mandy admitted. "And of course you were upset. You thought we forgot you."

"I did think that," Michelle admitted.

"You're too good a friend to lose, Michelle," Cassie said, slinging an arm over Michelle's shoulders. "We would never forget about you."

"Thanks," Michelle said. "And from now on I'll be an even better friend myself. Guaranteed."

Michelle ate her pizza, feeling better than she had in days.

"Hey, can I have some?" Evan, a boy in Michelle's class asked.

"Maybe later, Evan," Michelle answered.

"This was so nice of Stephanie to do," Cassie commented.

"We should do something nice for Stephanie in return," Mandy suggested.

"Please! No!" Michelle said through a mouthful of pizza. "That's what started this whole mess in the first place."

Cassie and Mandy laughed.

"Seriously," Mandy said. "What does Stephanie really, really want? Maybe we can help her get it."

Michelle thought about it. "She really wants to win this Challenge Day thing," she said.

The girls looked at one another. "I don't think there's any way we can help her with that," Cassie decided.

"Well," Michelle said, "she wants that kid Grant to like her again," Michelle told them. "There's nothing we can do about—"

She stopped talking. The beginning of a great idea had come into her head.

"What are you thinking?" Cassie asked.

"The first time I wrote to Grant I pretended I was Stephanie being nice. The second time I acted like Stephanie being mean. There's one thing I haven't tried."

"What?" Mandy asked.

"The truth," Michelle told them. "I never explained what really happened."

"Good idea," Mandy said, impressed.

"It's worth a try," Cassie agreed. "You could do it right now in the computer room."

Michelle, Cassie, and Mandy finished their slices. Then they stood up. "Free pizza while it lasts," she announced to the kids sitting nearby. A huge cheer went up from the table. A ton of Michelle's classmates crowded around the leftover pizza.

"Come on," Michelle told her friends.

They hurried into the computer room. In minutes Michelle was on the Internet, writing to Munsenman.

Hi, Grant, she wrote. *We met in the library. I'm Michelle, Stephanie Tanner's sister. There are some things I need to explain to you.*

From there she explained how she'd pretended to be Stephanie—both the nice Stephanie and the mean one.

Stephanie feels really bad about everything that's happened. She didn't use you to get the books back. My sister didn't even know I'd written to you. She's a very honest person, not someone who would play such a mean trick.

Michelle looked at her friends. "Anything else I should add?" she asked.

Cassie and Mandy thought.

"You could tell him she really likes him," Mandy suggested.

Michelle shook her head. "I'll leave that up to her."

"Then I think you've covered it," Cassie said.

"I guess so," Michelle agreed. She hit Send.

"He'll find that when he gets home from school today," Michelle said, getting up from her chair. "I just hope nothing too terrible happens between Grant and Stephanie before that."

Cassie crossed her fingers for luck.

"Double that," Mandy said, crossing her.

"Triple it," Michelle agreed, crossing her fingers, too. "And with triple power, we can't lose."

"Hey," Mandy replied, smiling. "That's what friends are for."

Stephanie

Chapter
15

Stephanie hurried straight home from school that afternoon. She wanted to make the final changes on her Egypt report.

They didn't take long. Stephanie stapled the pages together. She put them in a folder, then taped the map of Egypt on the front. "Done," she said, pleased.

This had been a lot of work. But she felt good about it. They had an excellent report to turn in on Monday.

Pushing her chair back, she looked at the books next to the computer. It would be a shame to just take them back to the library. So many other kids in her class could use them. Since Grant had renewed them, they weren't even due back for a while.

"Grant *is* the one who renewed them," she said quietly to herself. "The right thing would be to return them to him."

Stephanie scooped the books up into her arms. Then she stopped. She didn't want to *see* Grant, just give him the books. If they saw each other they might wind up fighting again.

Maybe she could ask Darcy or Allie to bring them over.

Then she remembered. Darcy was at a gymnastics practice for another hour. Allie had a piano lesson.

I might as well do it myself, she decided. *I'll leave them on his front steps and go.*

She looked up Grant's address in the directory. He didn't live far. If she went on her bike, she could be back in less than half an hour.

It took Stephanie just ten minutes to find her way to Grant's house. Her heart began to race as she climbed the front steps. *I hope these books will be safe here,* she worried.

Lifting her head, she checked the sky. No signs of rain. There wasn't even a wind. It would be safe to leave the books.

Stephanie placed them on the top step. She backed down the stairs, watching to see if they would blow or slip down the steps.

As she turned, Stephanie bumped right into Grant. He was carrying a brown bag full of groceries.

"Oh!" she cried. "Sorry. I didn't see you." She braced for the nasty remark she was sure he'd make.

"I wondered when you'd stop staring at my front door and turn around," he said. His voice was surprisingly pleasant.

Stephanie stared at him for a moment. "Oh, I wasn't staring at your door. I must have looked so silly. No. I was checking to make sure those books would be okay there."

He peered up the steps at them. "Are those the books on Egypt?" he asked.

She nodded. "I was done with them, and I

wanted you to have them back. They are yours, after all."

"Thanks," he said.

An uncomfortable silence came up. They stood, looking at each other. For a moment, neither said anything.

"Look," Stephanie began. "There's only one thing I want you to know. I didn't use you to get the books back. It wasn't even me you were talking to on the Internet. It was—"

"Michelle," Grant cut her off.

Stephanie was shocked. "How did you know?"

"Your sister e-mailed me today. She told me the whole thing," he explained.

Stephanie laughed lightly, shaking her head. "Poor Michelle. I really confused her. First I was mad at her for giving you the books. Then I was angry because she tried to get them back. After that, I chewed her out for being mean to you."

Grant smiled. "It's kind of funny, actually. All she was trying to do was help out. But every time she made a move, she got blasted for it."

"Oh, you don't know half of what's been going on between us," Stephanie told him. "I sent her a pizza today in school. It was a peace gesture. I don't know if it will be enough, though. I've given her a lot of grief lately."

"Kind of like the grief I've been giving you?" Grant asked.

Stephanie shrugged. "You were mad," she said.

Grant rolled his eyes. "Oh, man, was I ever mad. But I didn't like the way I acted." He sat on one of the steps and Stephanie sat beside him.

"I had an idea about your sculpture," he said. "I think I know what you should do with it."

"Recycle it?" Stephanie asked.

He laughed. "No. It's good. You're just having a structural problem you didn't expect."

"I have an idea how to fix it," Stephanie told him.

"I do, too," he said. "You just need to get

some lumber or broom poles. If you put one going straight up one leg and into the middle and another one through the arms, he should be stable."

"I don't know," Stephanie said, shaking her head doubtfully. "I'm afraid that would make him look too stiff. Your Century Man is a robot. He's supposed to be stiff. But John Muir was a real man—and a naturalist. He should look . . . well, natural."

"He's going to look dead if he can't stand up," Grant commented.

Stephanie laughed. "I was thinking that once we put his papier-mâché clothing on, that would make him steadier. And we can give him a walking stick, which will hold him up, too."

Stephanie had one more brand-new idea. For a moment she wondered if she should give her secret away to Grant. She decided to take a chance. "I want to put chimes and bells on him. Anything that makes a noise when it moves. That way his looseness will be a plus, not a problem. Every time he sways a little he'll make a nice sound. Don't you think it would be cool if he sort of chimes a little?"

"It would be," he agreed. "And hey, why don't you put him on some kind of big stand," Grant suggested. "It will make him look more—"

"Like Century Man?" she teased.

"Well . . . Century Man is pretty huge. A stand might kind of even things up, competitionwise."

Stephanie considered this. It wasn't a bad idea, but she didn't want to just plunk the sculpture on a box.

"It might be good if we built a sort of slope and had him climbing it, as if he were on a mountain path," Stephanie agreed.

"Yeah, you could put rocks and dirt and stuff at his feet—" Grant stopped short. "Hey, wait a minute. This is starting to sound better than Century Man."

"Right now Century Man is the frontrunner," Stephanie admitted. "You could stand some competition."

"You're right," he said. "As long as it's *friendly* competition."

"Agreed. Besides, the real goal is to make a cool sculpture for the school—not to win," Stephanie continued. "That's the idea we're really supposed to be getting behind."

"I know, but . . . Century Man still rules."

Stephanie dug into his arm lightly with her knuckle. "You had to get that in, didn't you?" she teased.

He laughed. "I can't help it. I'm competitive."

"Well, so am I," Stephanie responded. "And John Muir will take the prize."

"Century Man!" Grant shouted, punching the air.

"John Muir! John Muir!" Stephanie chanted.

They fell back, laughing at their own silliness.

Maybe this was how their relationship would always be—competitive. But at least now they were friendly rivals.

And perhaps in the future they'd be something more than that.

Stephanie headed for home feeling relieved and lighthearted. But as she neared her own front door, she began to worry.

Had Michelle accepted her pizza peace offering? Would they be able to patch things up and be friends the way they once were?

Michelle

Chapter
16

Michelle jumped up from her bed. Finally she heard it—the unmistakable sound of Stephanie coming through the front door.

Her sister always shut the door louder than anyone. Three steps to the phone machine, then it went on as Stephanie checked for messages. Yes, it was Stephanie, all right.

Putting down her book, Michelle hurried out of their room and to the stairs.

"Stephanie," she said when she was at the top of the stairs.

"Michelle," Stephanie said at the same time, their voices overlapping.

"Thanks for the pizza."

"Thanks for e-mailing Grant."

Once again, they spoke in unison.

They laughed at the sound of their mingled words.

"You'd better talk first," Stephanie suggested.

"Okay," Michelle agreed. "I guess Grant told you I sent an e-mail telling him the whole story."

Stephanie nodded. "Listen, Michelle, I know you've just been trying to help. I've been very impatient with you and I'm very sorry."

A warm feeling came over Michelle. These were the words she'd been dying to hear. "It's okay," she said. "I'm sorry all my plans backfired."

"The important thing is that you meant well," Stephanie assured her.

Michelle was so glad they were making up, though this wasn't completely over. She needed to ask an important question.

"So—what did I do to make you so mad that you wanted to stay away from me in the first place?" she asked.

A confused expression came over Stephanie's face. "Before you returned the library books? Nothing," she said.

"But that can't be," Michelle protested. "I read the letter you wrote to Dear Libby! I saw it in *Daisy* magazine. I know it was from you."

Stephanie dropped onto the couch. She looked completely stunned. "Oh, man. This is too much!" She shook her head from side to side.

"What?" Michelle asked.

"You saw the letter *I* wrote to *Daisy*?" Stephanie asked. "You mean the one from the girl with the huge family that couldn't stand her sister?"

"Yeah," Michelle responded.

"Michelle, I thought *you* wrote that letter," Stephanie told her. "In fact, I was sure you did. That's why I was trying to give you some space. That's what Libby said to do."

"She also suggested being extra nice,"

Michelle reminded her. "That's what *I* was trying to do."

Stephanie held her forehead with the palm of her hand. "Wow! What a couple of idiots we are. Neither of us wrote that letter. Which means neither of us had a problem with the other to begin with."

Michelle plopped down on the couch beside Stephanie. What a relief. "How could you think I'd write something like that?" she asked her sister. "I love sharing a room with you."

"Same here," Stephanie agreed.

They put their arms around each other and hugged. "Let's never fight again, okay?" Michelle asked.

"You've got a deal, little sister," Stephanie agreed.

At that moment Danny walked in from the kitchen. "Thank goodness!" he cheered. "Do my eyes deceive me, or are things finally back to normal around here?"

"Totally back to normal," Michelle reported. "And Dad, wait until you hear what's been going on. It all started when our *Daisy* magazine came last week."

Michelle explained the whole story. Stephanie jumped in here and there to add information.

Danny shook his head, rolled his eyes, and chuckled as the tale unfolded.

"And we just this minute discovered that neither one of us wrote the letter. Can you believe it?" Michelle ended.

Stephanie looked at Michelle. "We should tell all this to Libby."

"Great idea," Michelle agreed. "She'd probably get a good laugh out of it."

Stephanie checked her watch. "The chat is just about to start. We can get in at the beginning, if you want."

"Let's go." Michelle jumped off the couch.

"It's great to see you girls doing something together again," Danny commented.

"Definitely," Stephanie agreed, following Michelle up the stairs.

At the computer Michelle got herself and Stephanie to the "Dear Libby" chat room.

"Have we ever got a story to tell you!" Michelle entered the chat. *"I say 'we' because my sister and I are writing this together. Just last week we thought we'd never do anything together again. Luckily, we were wrong—about a lot of things. And it all started with your column."*

Dear Libby replied, *"This sounds interesting. Tell us all about it."*

"Squish in here," Michelle told her sister. She slid over in her chair to give Stephanie some room. Together the two of them took turns telling their tale of misunderstanding.

"I have something to tell you girls," Libby wrote when they'd finished. *"That letter you thought your sister wrote—came from Peoria, Illinois!"*

Stephanie and Michelle read the line and collapsed onto each other, laughing.

Michelle knew that she and Stephanie were not just sisters, but friends once again.

*Don't miss out on any of
Stephanie and Michelle's
exciting adventures!*

FULL HOUSE™
Sisters

**When sisters get together...
expect the unexpected!**

A MINSTREL® BOOK

Published by Pocket Books

2012-05

FULL HOUSE™
Michelle

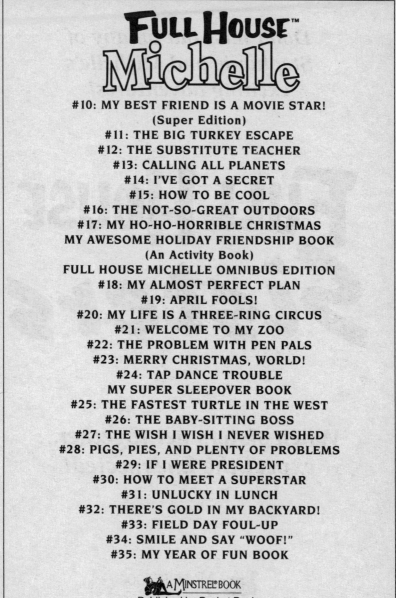

#10: MY BEST FRIEND IS A MOVIE STAR!
(Super Edition)
#11: THE BIG TURKEY ESCAPE
#12: THE SUBSTITUTE TEACHER
#13: CALLING ALL PLANETS
#14: I'VE GOT A SECRET
#15: HOW TO BE COOL
#16: THE NOT-SO-GREAT OUTDOORS
#17: MY HO-HO-HORRIBLE CHRISTMAS
MY AWESOME HOLIDAY FRIENDSHIP BOOK
(An Activity Book)
FULL HOUSE MICHELLE OMNIBUS EDITION
#18: MY ALMOST PERFECT PLAN
#19: APRIL FOOLS!
#20: MY LIFE IS A THREE-RING CIRCUS
#21: WELCOME TO MY ZOO
#22: THE PROBLEM WITH PEN PALS
#23: MERRY CHRISTMAS, WORLD!
#24: TAP DANCE TROUBLE
MY SUPER SLEEPOVER BOOK
#25: THE FASTEST TURTLE IN THE WEST
#26: THE BABY-SITTING BOSS
#27: THE WISH I WISH I NEVER WISHED
#28: PIGS, PIES, AND PLENTY OF PROBLEMS
#29: IF I WERE PRESIDENT
#30: HOW TO MEET A SUPERSTAR
#31: UNLUCKY IN LUNCH
#32: THERE'S GOLD IN MY BACKYARD!
#33: FIELD DAY FOUL-UP
#34: SMILE AND SAY "WOOF!"
#35: MY YEAR OF FUN BOOK

A MINSTREL® BOOK
Published by Pocket Books

1033-34